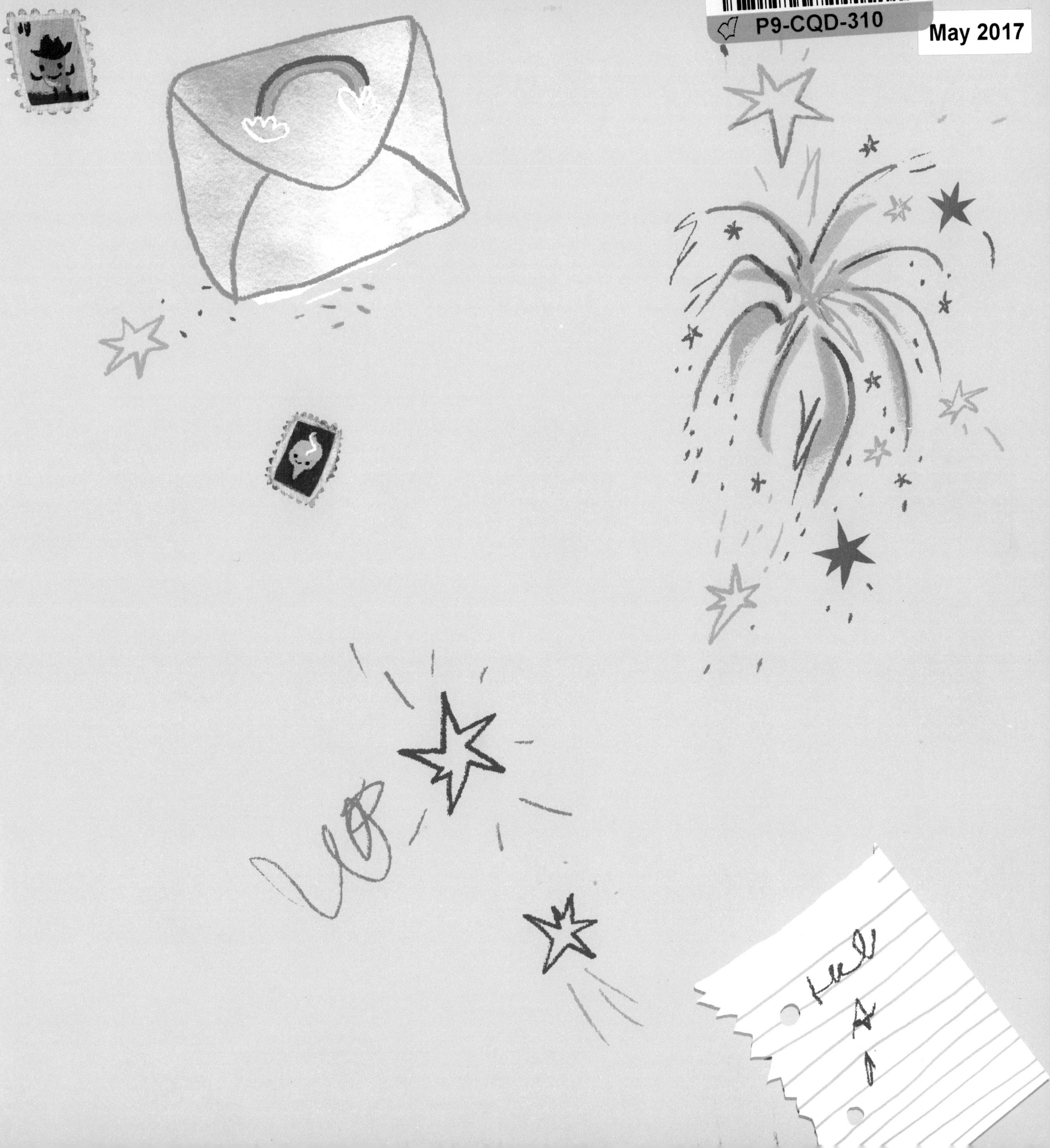

From

Here

To

There

SUE FLIESS

pictures by
Christiane Engel

ALBERT WHITMAN & COMPANY
Chicago, Illinois

To Owen and Wyatt, I'll always be here for you.—SF
To Maya—CE

Library of Congress Cataloging-in-Publication
data is on file with the publisher.

Text copyright © 2016 by Sue Fliess
Pictures copyright © 2016 by Albert Whitman & Company
Pictures by Christiane Engel
Published in 2016 by Albert Whitman & Company
ISBN 978-0-8075-2622-4
Printed in China
10 9 8 7 6 5 4 3 2 1 LP 20 19 18 17 16
Design by Jordan Kost

For more information about Albert Whitman & Company,
visit our web site at www.albertwhitman.com.

Here and There were so much alike
they were practically twins.

But they could never be together
because Here was always Here,

and There was always There.

"Come over, Here!" called There.

"Sorry, I can't go, There!" cried Here.

But they weren't going to let distance
come between them.

So they became pen pals.

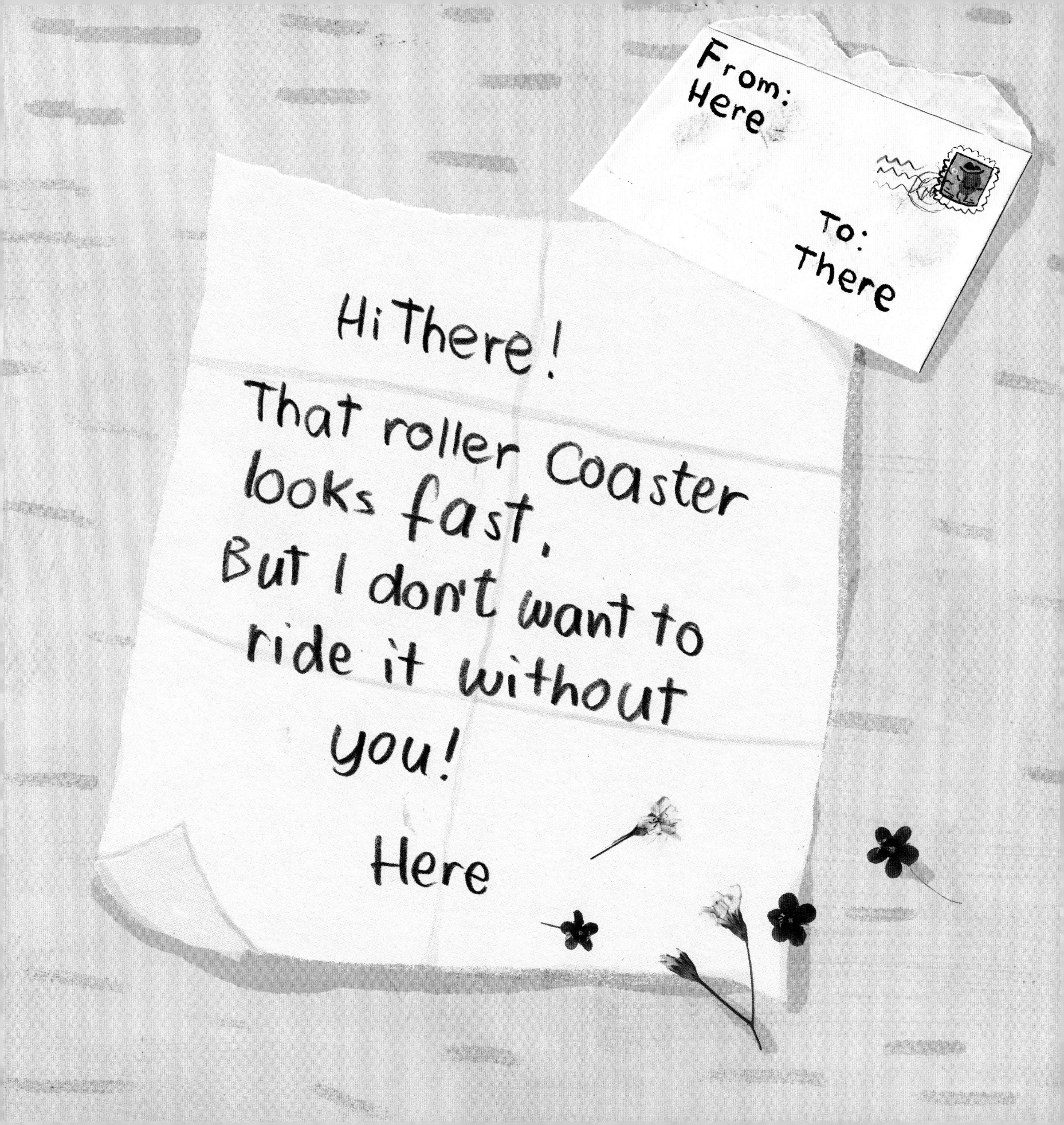
From:
Here
To:
There
Hi There!
That roller coaster looks fast.
But I don't want to ride it without you!
Here

Dear Here,
The haunted house looks scary! I wish you could go through it with me.
There
From: There
To: Here

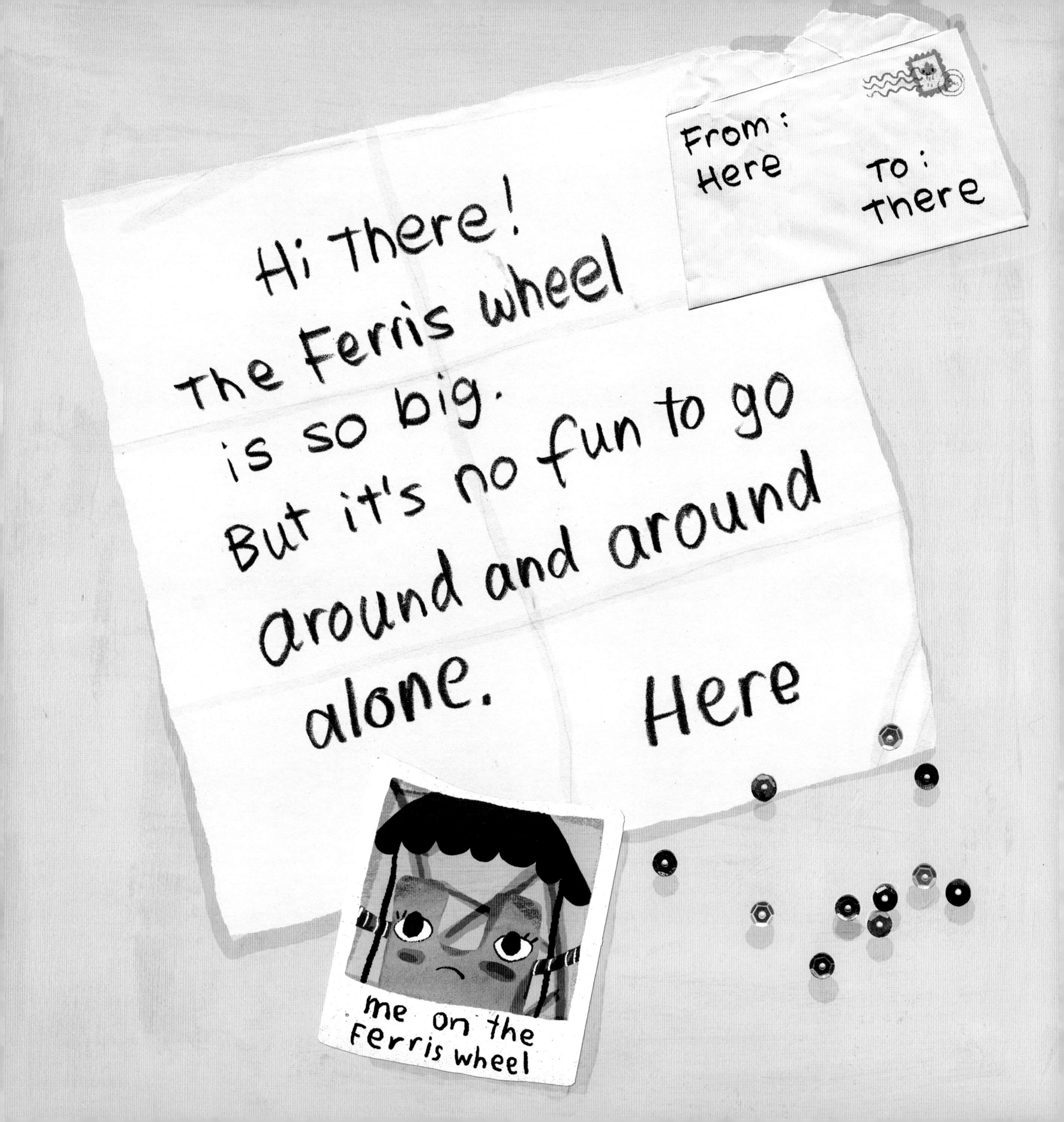

Hi There!
The Ferris wheel is so big.
But it's no fun to go around and around alone.

Here

me on the Ferris wheel

Watching the giant wheel turn
gave There an idea.

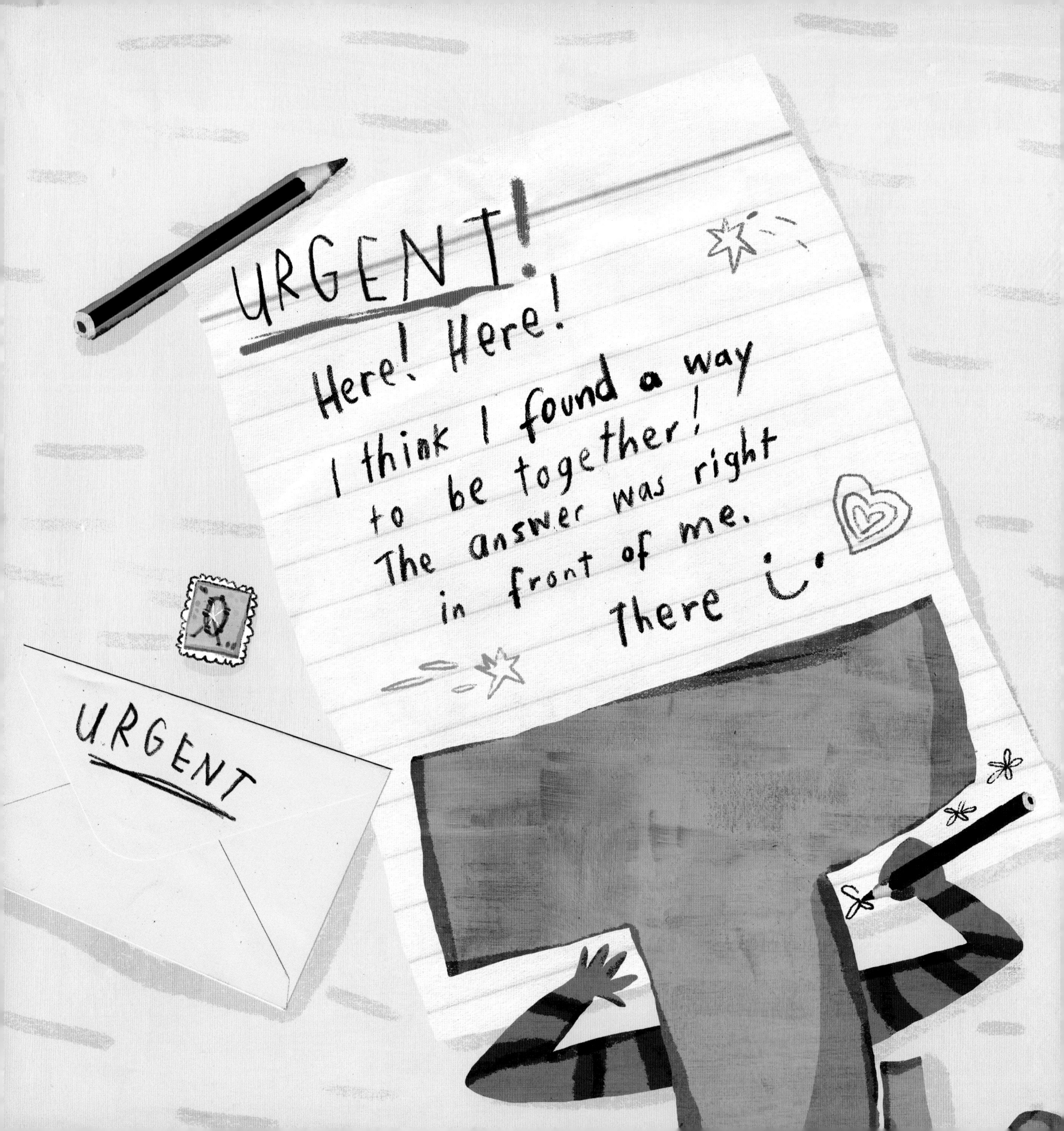
URGENT!
Here! Here!
I think I found a way
to be together!
The answer was right
in front of me.
There
URGENT

Here thought about the roller coaster and the haunted house and the Ferris wheel. She thought about There. Would they finally be together? She was so excited she could barely sleep.

There got to work on his idea right away.

He tinkered and toiled
through the night.

"Terrific!"

"There?" asked Here.

There laughed.
"I'm Here now!"

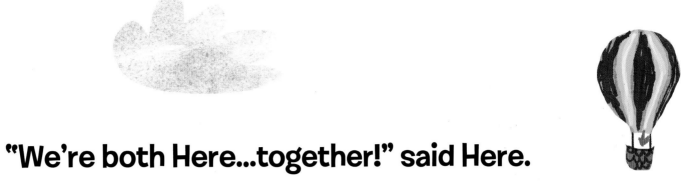

"We're both Here...together!" said Here.

The two friends climbed up and raced down,

held hands through,

and rode around
and around,

together.

But soon it was time to go.

"We both knew
I couldn't stay
Here forever,"
said There.

"I'll be Here
whenever you
need me."

"Even when you're There and I'm Here, we'll find a way to be together," said Here.

And the two friends knew they were
never more than one letter apart.

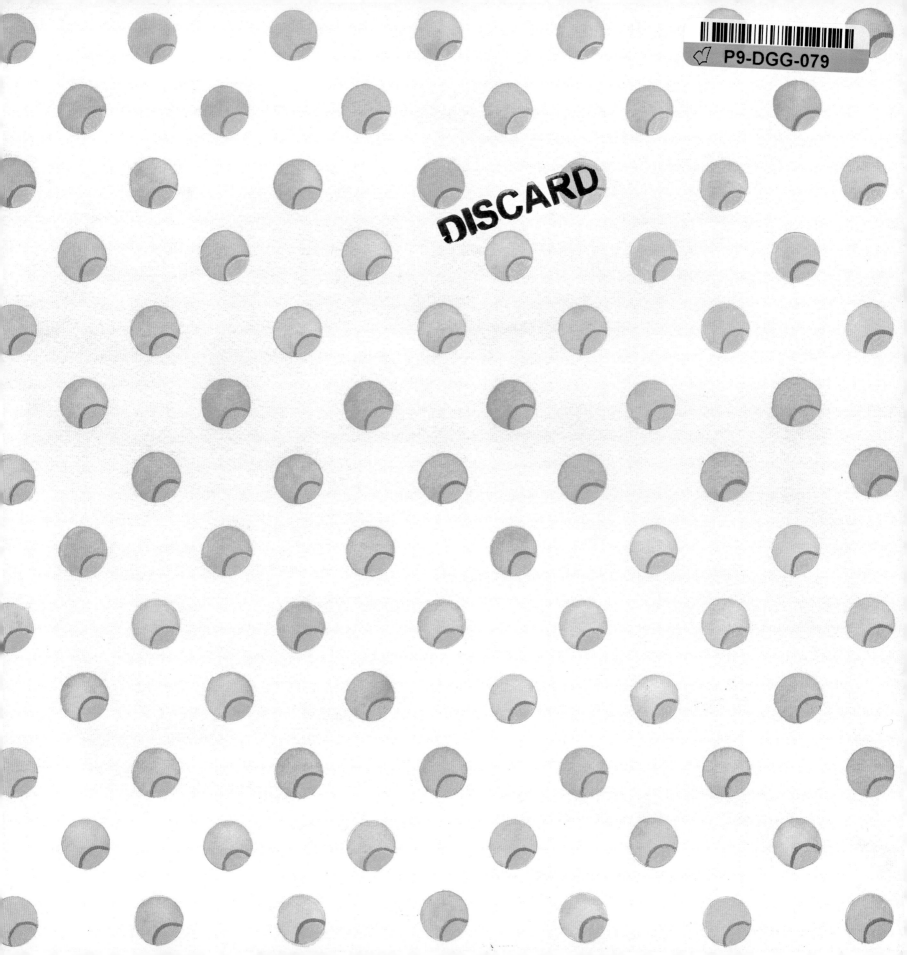

This book is your book. I wrote it for you. —Love, S.L.-J.

For Elizabeth, with love —J.D.

Visit us on the Web! randomhouse.com/kids
Educators and librarians, for a variety of teaching tools, visit us at RHTeachersLibrarians.com

Library of Congress Cataloging-in-Publication Data
Lloyd-Jones, Sally. The house that's your home / by Sally Lloyd-Jones ;
illustrated by Jane Dyer. – First edition.
pages cm
Summary: Celebrates all the things that make one's home special,
including the family that dwells there.
ISBN 978-0-375-85884-0 (hc) – ISBN 978-0-375-95884-7 (glb) – ISBN 978-0-375-98798-4 (ebook)
[1. Home—Fiction. 2. Family life—Fiction.] 1. Dyer, Jane, illustrator. II. Title. III. Title: House that is your home.
PZ7.L77878Hm 2015   [E]–dc23   2014005641

The text of this book is set in Jane Dyer's hand lettering.
The illustrations are rendered in gouache and pencil on 140-lb. cold press paper.
MANUFACTURED IN CHINA
2 4 6 8 10 9 7 5 3 1
First Edition

The House that's Your Home

by Sally Lloyd-Jones

illustrated by Jane Dyer

schwartz & wade books · new york

A girl is a Daughter

And a boy is a Son

And a mommy is Your Mommy

And a daddy is Your Daddy

And you are a Family

Together

In the house that's Your Home.

A cat is Your Cat
And a dog is Your Dog
And they are Your Pets.

Up the stairs is a room

With Your Name on its door

That's the room of Your Own

In the house that's Your Home

With a window to show you the sky.

A book is Your Book
And a ball is Your Ball
And they are Your Things.

And the shoes on your feet

That you use when you stomp

Are to carry you out

Of the door of the house

That's Your Home.

A field is Your Yard,

The grass where you play.

And the ground is a bed

For the seeds that you grew

Into poppies and peas

And fiddlehead ferns

For the garden of Your Own

Of the house that's Your Home.

A tree is Your Tree
That stands in Your Yard,
Your place where you go
That's holding Your Swing
And listening
Quietly
For you.

And your Swing is to swing you

Right up to the sky,

Up over the wall,

Up, up, till you see

Swallows and cornfields

And tractors and sheep

And the world that is waiting below.

Look! There is Your Garden!
Your Window!
Your Room!
There is the roof
Of the house that's Your Home!

A bike is Your Bike
That rides you around.

A hoop is Your Hoop
That leads you along.

A bear is Your Bear
That follows behind.

A friend is Your Friend
Who stays by your side
And chooses you first
And saves you a place.

And Your Hands are to build

And Your Legs are to run

And Your Voice is to shout

Your Song to the skies

And Your Face is to turn to the sun.

And the stones on the ground
Are a path for Your Feet
To carry you back
To the door of the house
That's Your Home.

A chair is Your Chair

Where you sit when you eat

With a plate for Your Food

And a cup for Your Juice

With the Family you love

In the house that's Your Home.

A grandma is Your Grandma
And a grandpa is Your Grandpa
And their legs won't go fast
And they're all full of years
But their stories are strong
And their hearts are so big
And they love you so much
That they can't ever stop.
And they belong to each other
And to you.

A bed is Your Bed
That's a ship to the moon,
To the space of the sky
That is holding the stars
And the vast Milky Way
And the dreams
That belong
Just to You.

And the moon shines down on
Your Bed as you sleep
In the room of Your Own
In the house that's Your Home.

And the sun rising up
Is the light of Your Eyes

And Your Heart is a bed

For the YOU that will grow

All the days of Your Life

In the air that you breathe

On the ground where you stand

In a place of Your Own

In the world

That's Your Home.

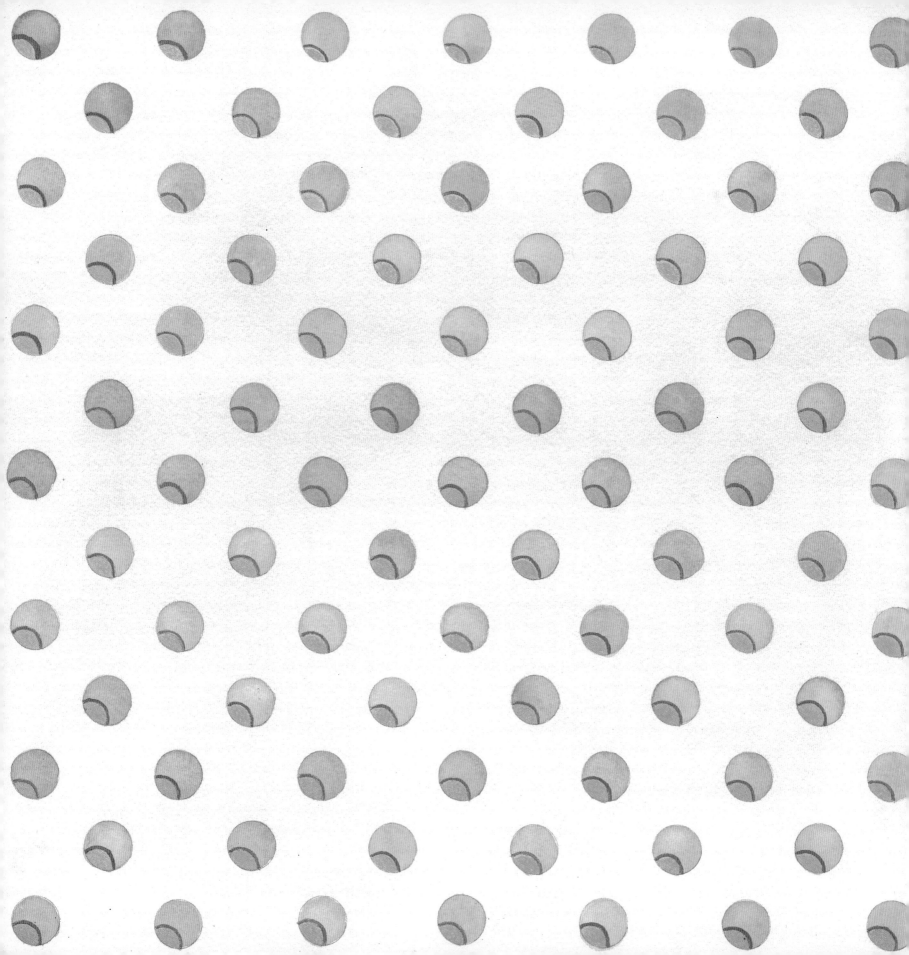